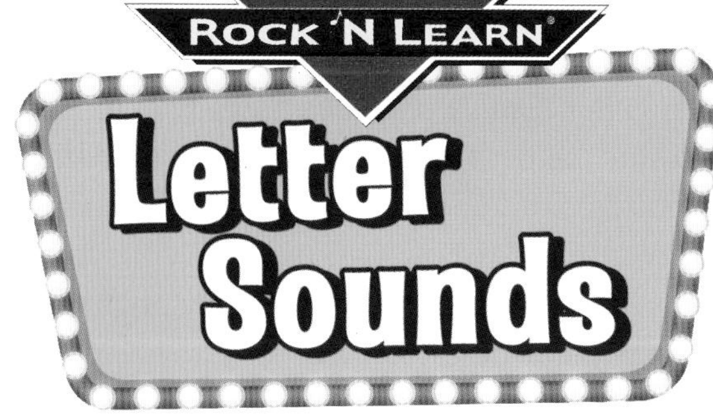

Vocal performances by:
D.J. Doc Roc
Tom McCain
Patti Bunyard
Shelly King

Spoken voices by:
Brad Caudle
Eric Leikam
Susan Rand
Christy Lynn
Tom Carter

Musical performances by:
Brad Caudle

Cover Design by:
Windy Polasek

Cover Illustration by:
Randy Rogers

Illustrations by:
Anthony Guerra
Bart Harlan

Written and produced by:
Brad Caudle
Melissa Caudle
Richard Caudle

Speech consultation by:
Denise Cloyd
Donna Mann
Tana Wade

www.rocknlearn.com

Instructional Guide

Rock 'N Learn *Letter Sounds* provides a fun way to learn the most common sound made by each letter of the alphabet. After learning these sounds, students practice putting them together to make words. They also learn how two or more consonants can be combined to make other sounds in words (consonant blends along with one consonant digraph: ck).

Although *Letter Sounds* is not intended to be a complete reading program, it introduces learners to some basic phonics rules and offers practice reading simple words and short sentences. As a follow-up to *Letter Sounds*, Rock 'N Learn *Phonics Volumes I & II* provide more advanced phonics instruction. These programs are also available on DVD video.

Tips for Success

Students listen to the audio and follow along with the book. Repeated exposure allows them to join in with the audio. After practicing skills learned on the first portions of the program, learners will be ready to advance. Should a particular song seem difficult, repeat that song as often as necessary. Learners may need assistance in locating the segments appropriate for their skill level.

Consider the attention span of young students. Learning sessions need not be lengthy to be effective. Practicing one or two songs per session may be plenty.

It's always a good idea to read a variety of books to children, beginning at an early age. Children who have adults read to them on a regular basis become better readers themselves. Obtain library cards, and explore the fun reading programs offered by your local library.

THE NEW ALPHABET SONG

A B C D E F
G H I J K L
M N O P Q R
S T U V W X
Y Z

a b c d e f g
h i j k l m n
o p q r s t u
v w x y z

LEARN THE SOUNDS

A a apple	B b bug
C c cat	D d dog

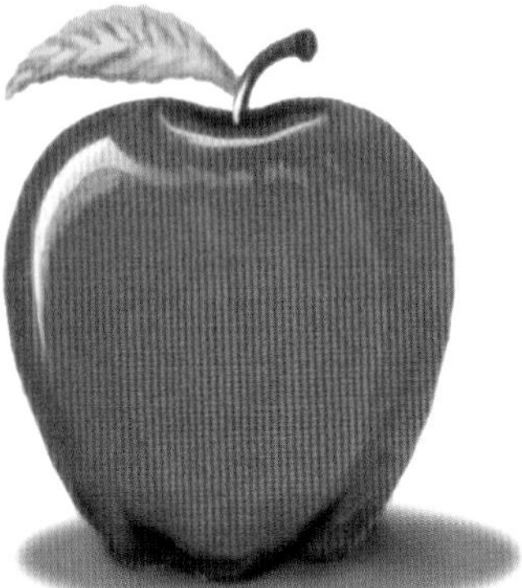

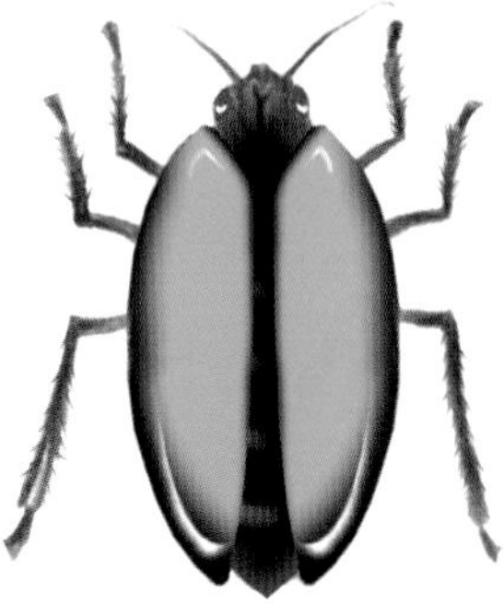

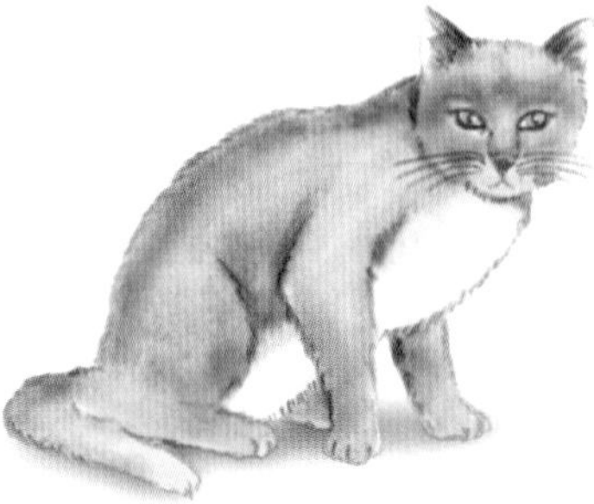

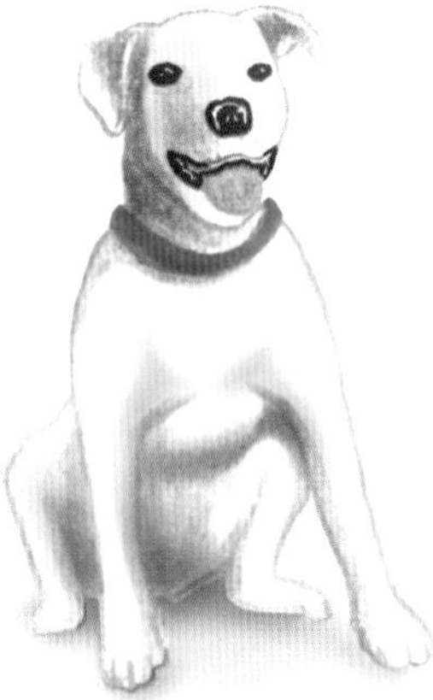

Ee egg	Ff fan
Gg gum	Hh hat

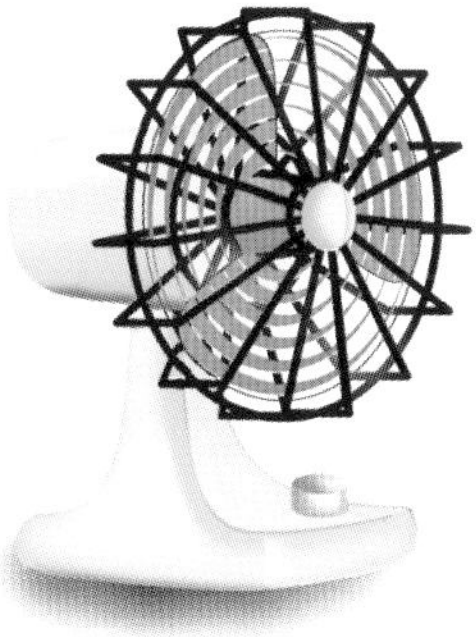

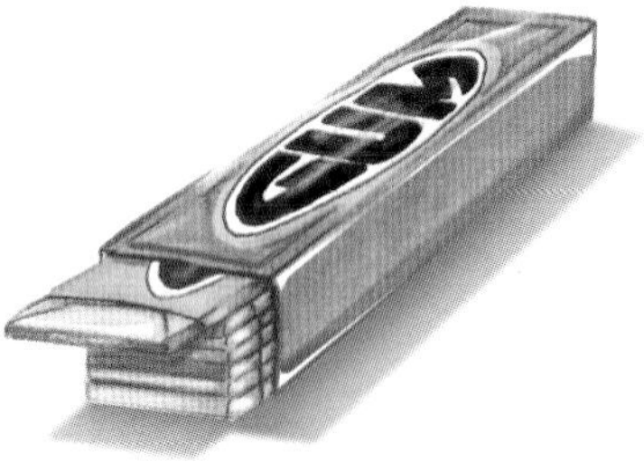

4

Mm mug	Nn nut
Oo octopus	**Pp** pig

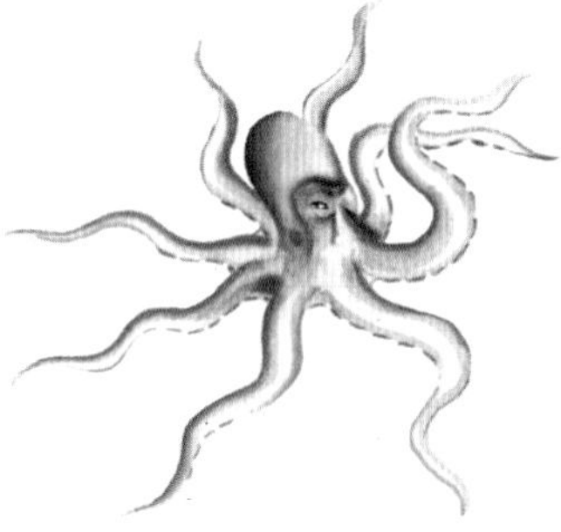

6

Qq	Rr
quilt	rat
Ss	Tt
sun	top

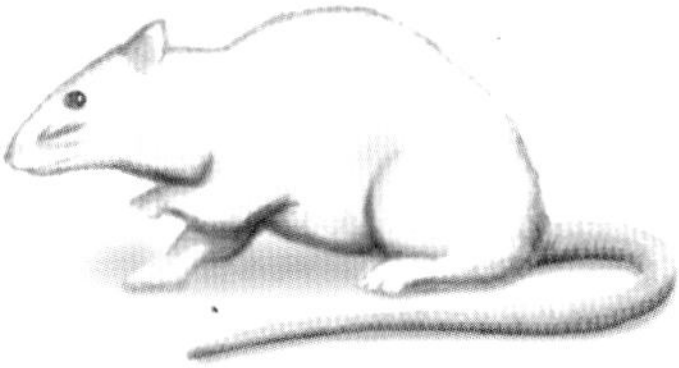

Uu umbrella	**Vv** van
Ww well	**Xx** fox

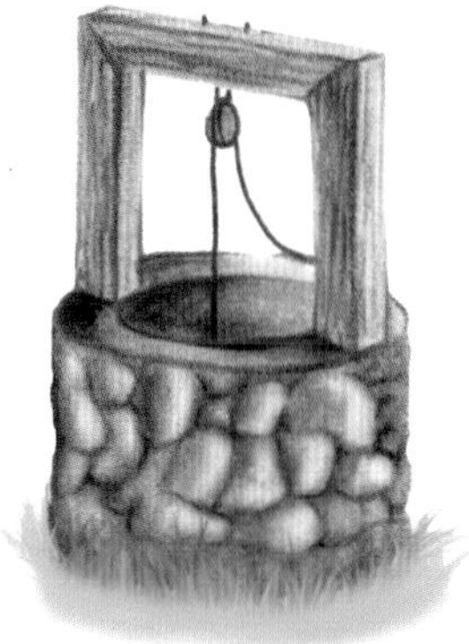

LETTER SOUNDS QUIZ Play this game with the book closed.

NAME THAT LETTER

Listen for the letter heard most in each sentence. Find the picture that matches each sentence.

9

READING WORDS

h hat   a apple   d dog

h a d   had

A a	an	as	at
B b	bus	bed	big
C c	cop	cut	can
D d	dip	dug	dad
E e	egg	Ed	

F f	fit	fed	fun
G g	gas	get	got
H h	had	hot	him
I i	it	if	in
J j	jog	job	jug
K k	kiss	kid	kit
L l	lip	lot	log

⑫

M m	met	mop	man
N n	nap	nut	not
O o	ox	on	off
P p	pet	pop	pan
Q q	quiz	quit	
R r	run	red	ran
S s	sun	sit	sad

F f	fit	fed	fun
G g	gas	get	got
H h	had	hot	him
I i	it	if	in
J j	jog	job	jug
K k	kiss	kid	kit
L l	lip	lot	log

⑫

M m	met	mop	man
N n	nap	nut	not
O o	ox	on	off
P p	pet	pop	pan
Q q	quiz	quit	
R r	run	red	ran
S s	sun	sit	sad

T t	ten	top	tag
U u	us	up	
V v	vet	van	vat
W w	wet	win	wag
X x	mix	box	fix
Y y	yet	yes	yam
Z z	zip	zig	zag

14

WORDS WITH CONSONANT COMBINATIONS

Some words are short.
Some words are long.
Put the sounds together
and read along.

You can sound out
words in this song.
Keep practicing and
you can't go wrong.

br a t	brat
cl a p	clap
cr a b	crab
fl a g	flag
gl a ss	glass
gr a ss	grass
sn a p	snap
tr a p	trap
l a mp	lamp
qu a ck	quack
a nt	ant
a sk	ask
l a st	last
h a nd	hand

You're doing good.
You're doing fine.
Look at page 15
and stay in time.

bl e ss	bless
l e ft	left
e lf	elf
e lk	elk
e lm	elm
h e lp	help
m e lt	melt
s e nd	send
s e nt	sent
w e nt	went
k e pt	kept
d e sk	desk
r e st	rest
t e st	test

You know the sounds
that you will need.
Turn to page 16
and learn to read.

fl i p	flip
sk i p	skip
sl i p	slip
sp i n	spin
spl i t	split
st i ll	still
sw i m	swim
tr i p	trip
tw i st	twist
m i lk	milk
qu i ck	quick
qu i lt	quilt
h i nt	hint
l i st	list

Put letters together
and you can read.
It's easy, just look
at page 17.

bl o ck	block
cr o p	crop
dr o p	drop
fr o g	frog
sm o g	smog
sp o t	spot
st o p	stop
tr o t	trot
l o ck	lock
s o ft	soft
g o lf	golf
h o nk	honk
l o st	lost
st o mp	stomp

Turn to page 18 and
read some more.
You're reading better
than ever before.

cl u b	club
dr u m	drum
gr u b	grub
pl u m	plum
str u m	strum
d u ck	duck
g u lp	gulp
b u mp	bump
j u mp	jump
j u nk	junk
st u nk	stunk
s u nk	sunk
m u st	must
j u st	just

MEMORY WORDS

the of for

see go to

them that you

is has then

this there do

was my from

Note: Some words on this page can be sounded with knowledge of other phonics rules such as those taught in *Rock 'N Learn Phonics.* However, given only the rules of this program, learners ed to memorize these words by sight to read the sentences on pages 20–28. *Rock 'N Learn nics* is recommended for use after *Letter Sounds.*

A frog sat on a log.

The log was in a pond.

The frog can jump.

The frog is off the log.

A cat slept on a mat.

A dog sat on the cat.

The cat ran from the dog.

The dog slept on the mat.

I can clap.

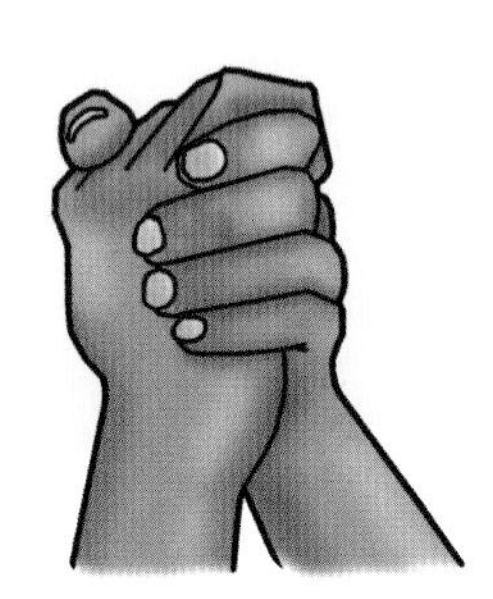

You can snap.

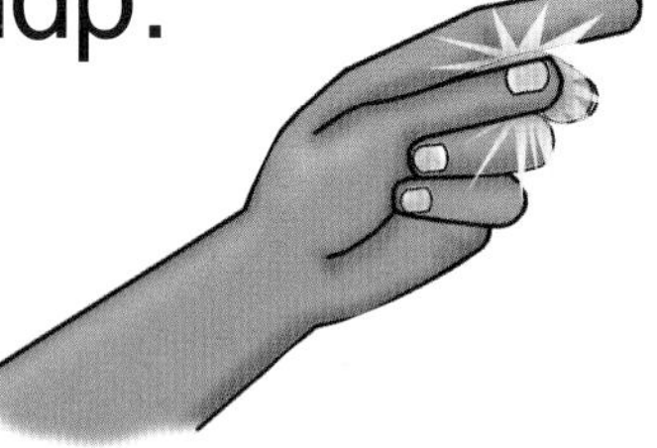

Dad can tap the drum.

Bob will rap.

I ran fast.

I fell.

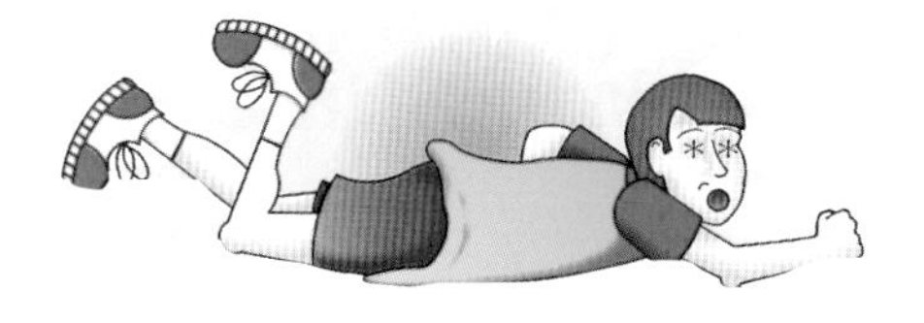

I cut my leg.

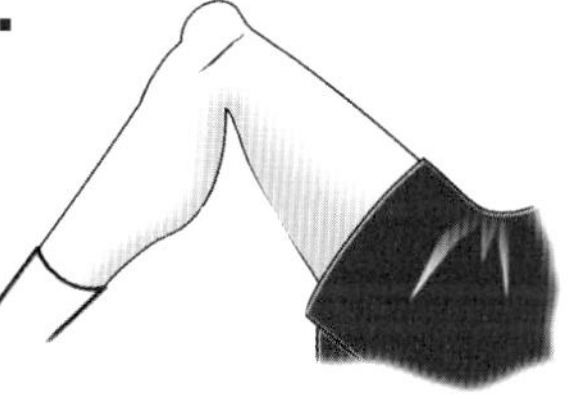

Jan got help.

I can kick a can.

The can will spin.

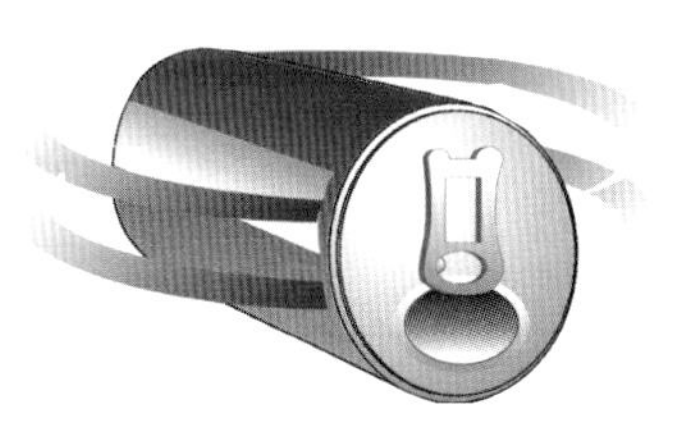

Then the can will stop.

Did you see the duck?

See it swim in the pond.

It will quack.

The dog was lost.

I will lift the quilt.

The dog will jump up.

The dog will lick my hand.

Bob can see the ant run.

The ant ran fast.

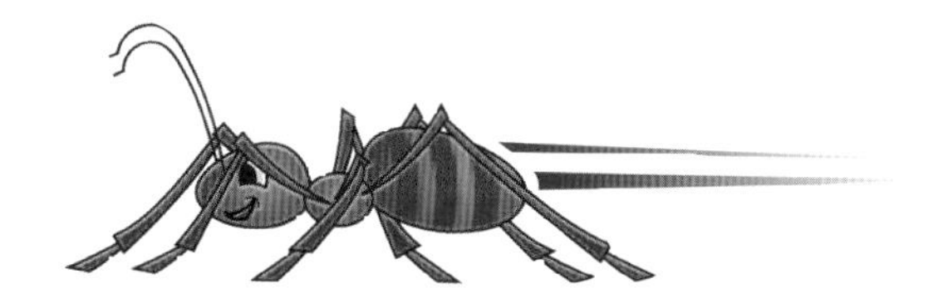

Bob will ask Nan to see the ant.

Nan and Bob will see it run.

Mom can run.

Dad can jog.

I will skip fast.

The New Alphabet Song

ABCDEFGHIJKLMNOPQRSTUVWXYZ

Alphabet Song
That's right, we're playin' it.
And the alphabet
Soon you'll be sayin' it.
Say the letters along with me.
You can learn your ABC's.

ABCDEFGHIJKLMNOPQRSTUVWXYZ

Now that you've heard this alphabet song
Let's go a little faster while you sing along.
Sing along with a happenin' beat
While you're learnin' your ABC's.

ABCDEFGHIJKLMNOPQRSTUVWXYZ

ABCDEFGHIJKLMNOPQRSTUVWXYZ

Learning To Read

Learning to read and we're reading to learn.
We've read together, and now it's your turn.

If you will practice, you can learn to read.
At first we read slowly, but then we gain speed.

Learning to read can be easy and fun.
Let's keep on reading 'cause we've just begun.

You can read signs or books that are long.
You can read poems or words to a song.

You can read postcards or rules to a game.
Once you learn reading, it's all just the same.

Cereal boxes and packages too.
Reading will open the world up to you.

Just keep on reading; each day you will find
That you are growing a strong, healthy mind.

Read about all the fun things you can do.
Read about animals found in a zoo.

Read about planets, the moon, and the stars.
Read about airplanes, trains, boats, and cars.

Now go find something that is good to read.
We got you started; now you take the lead!

Silly Sentences

An alligator and an ant added apples.

Jolly jellyfish jump for joy.

Cute cuddly cats crunch cucumbers.

Zany zebras zigzag at the zoo.

Nice nanny goats never noticed new neon necklaces.

Darling dogs danced daintily in the daisies.

Impolite insects ignore icky inchworms.

Bouncing boys break beds before bedtime.

Kind kangaroos kiss koalas.

Eddie enjoys extra eggs every morning.

Many monkeys make mailmen mad.

Two turtles toppled twenty tulips.

Funny Freddy fried five fish for food.

Hungry horses hate having hiccups.

Polly Porcupine pokes people.

Volcanoes vibrate very vocal vultures.

Sweaty socks sometimes smell stinky.

Your yellow yams are yummy.

Ollie Octopus often objects to olives.

Grumpy gorillas grab gorgeous girls.

Rough rats run rowdy races.

Ugly umbrellas unexpectedly open up.

Lovely lions leap over lazy leopards.

Willie watches Wilma Walrus walk wonderfully.

Quaint queens quietly quit quilting.

The fox will fix box six.

ROCK 'N LEARN

More Programs

Early Learning
Nursery Rhymes (CD/book, DVD or VHS)
Colors, Shapes & Counting (CD/book, DVD or VHS)
Alphabet (CD/book, DVD or VHS)
Alphabet Circus (DVD or VHS)
Alphabet Exercise (DVD or VHS)
Animals (DVD or VHS)
Getting Ready for Kindergarten (DVD or VHS)

Reading
Letter Sounds (CD/book, DVD or VHS)
Phonics (CD/book, DVD or VHS)
Phonics Easy Readers on DVD

Foreign Languages
Spanish I (CD/book), Spanish II (CD/book)
Spanish I & II (DVD or VHS)
French I (CD/book)

Math
Addition Rap (CD/book)
Subtraction Rap (CD/book)
Addition & Subtraction Rap (DVD or VHS)
Addition & Subtraction Rock (CD/book, DVD or VHS)
Addition & Subtraction Country (CD/book)
Multiplication Rap (CD/book, DVD or VHS)
Multiplication Rock (CD/book, DVD or VHS)
Multiplication Country (CD/book)
Division Rap (CD/book, DVD or VHS)
Division Rock (CD/book)
Money & Making Change (DVD or VHS)
Telling Time (DVD or VHS)
Beginning Fractions & Decimals (DVD or VHS)

& More!
Dinosaur Rap (CD/book)
Solar System (CD/book)
Presidents & U.S. Government (CD/book)
States & Capitals Rap (CD/book)
Grammar (CD/book)

Call 800-348-8445 or 936-539-2731
Or visit www.rocknlearn.com